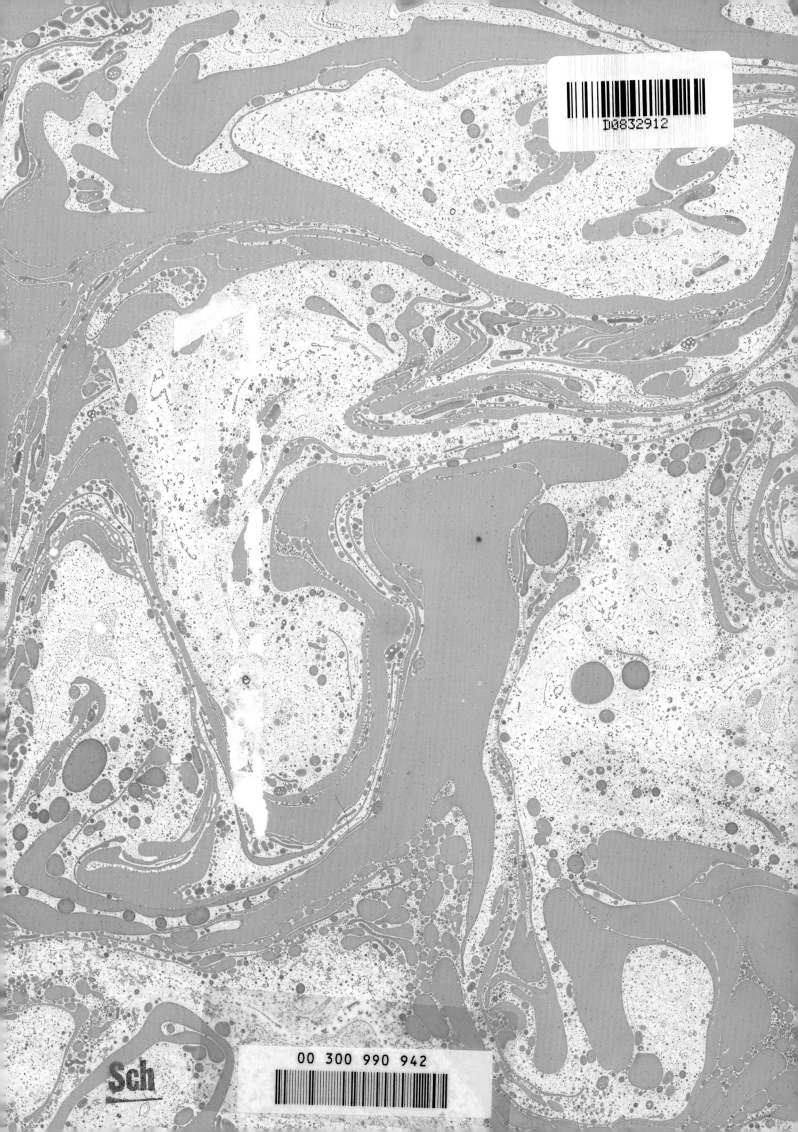

Sch

00 300 990 942

D0832912

For my excellent funky friend Diana, with much love ~V.F.

For my children, Zoë and Oska ~ K.P.

Marbled endpapers by Susan Moxley

Northamptonshire Libraries & Information Service	
Peters	05-Mar-98
CF	£12.99

VIKING

Published by the Penguin Group

Penguin Putnam Inc., 375 Hudson Street, New York, New York 10014, U.S.A.

Penguin Books Ltd, 27 Wrights Lane, London W8 5TZ, England

Penguin Books Australia Ltd, Ringwood, Victoria, Australia

Penguin Books Canada Ltd, 10 Alcorn Avenue, Toronto, Ontario, Canada M4V 3B2

Penguin Books (N.Z.) Ltd, 182 – 190 Wairau Road, Auckland 10, New Zealand

Penguin Books Ltd, Registered Offices: Harmondsworth, Middlesex, England

First published in Great Britain by Viking, a division of Penguin Books Ltd, 1997

First published in the U.S.A. by Viking, a member of Penguin Putnam Inc., 1998

1 3 5 7 9 10 8 6 4 2

Text copyright © Vivian French, 1997

Illustrations copyright © Korky Paul, 1997

Without limiting the rights under copyright reserved above, no part of this
publication may be reproduced, stored in or introduced into a retrieval system,
or transmitted, in any form or by any means (electronic, mechanical,
photocopying, recording or otherwise), without the prior written permission
of both the copyright owner and the above publisher of this book.

ISBN 0-670-87524-4

AESOP'S FUNKY FABLES

Retold by Vivian French

Illustrated by Korky Paul

VIKING

Who was Aesop?

Aesop was a slave.

He lived in Greece on the isle of Samos.

When did he live?

Many years ago.

How many years? A thousand years?

Add another thousand, then five hundred…

TWO THOUSAND FIVE HUNDRED YEARS AGO?

That's right.

What did he do and what did he look like?

Was he a slave for all of his life?

Some say Aesop was a short man, an ugly man

Some say he stammered and he stuttered when he spoke

Some say he won his freedom with his stories

Some say he won his freedom with a joke.

Some say his master was a man called Xanthus

Some say Xanthus at last set him free

And he packed up his words in his bag and he travelled

Over the mountains, over the sea.

Aesop's story ended at Delphi

Some say priests there threw him to his death

Aesop told them a final story

It was words words words with his final breath…

Words + words + words + words + words = STORIES

CONTENTS

THE FOX AND THE CROW

Once upon a time there was a fox
(Fox fox fox fox fox fox fox)
And he lived in the woods
(In the woods, in the woods)
And he was always hungry.

He ate and he ate 'til his jaws were sore
And he ate and he ate and he ate a little more
Then he crunched up the bones and he licked his paw
And he said
"I'm hungry!"
And he moaned and he groaned and he mumbled and
    he grumbled
And he rolled on his belly and his belly rumbled
And he said
"I'm SO hungry!"

So he went for a walk in the woods
(In the woods, in the woods)
And up in a tree he saw a crow.
Blue black crow
Big shining beetle back blue black crow.
And crow had something in his beak
Something that smelled good
Something that smelled wonderful
Something that made fox lick his lips and drool.
YUM YUM YUM YUM YUM YUM YUM!
Sniff sniff sniff sniff sniff sniff sniff
"CHEESE!!!!
Oh my!" said the fox
(Fox fox fox fox fox fox fox)
"Oh me! Oh my!
If I don't get that cheese to eat
I'll die!

HEY, BROTHER CROW!
CAN YOU SEE ME HERE BELOW?"
The crow looked down at the fox
(Fox fox fox fox fox fox fox)
And he shook his head
And he kept his beak shut
And he winked his little bright eye
And he said
Nothing at all.
Then the fox
(Fox fox fox fox fox fox fox)
Sat down under the tree.

"OH, BROTHER CROW
I AM SIGHING
I AM CRYING
I AM DYING
FOR THE SOUND OF YOUR WONDERFUL
    VOICE.
BROTHER CROW
SING ME A SONG
WITH YOUR BEAUTIFUL FEATHERS ALL
    GLOSSY AND BLACK
WITH A SHEEN OF PURPLE ON YOUR HEAD
    AND YOUR BACK
WITH YOUR CLAWS AND YOUR BEAK AND
    YOUR TWINKLING EYE
SING ME A SONG BEFORE I DIE."

Brother Crow
Puffed up his feathers with pride
Puffed up his feathers
Puffed up
Puffed
And opened his beak wide
"CAW!" said the crow
"CAW!"
"Ho ho!" said the fox
(Fox fox fox fox fox fox fox)
As the cheese fell down to the ground.
"THANKS FOR THE CHEESE!" said the fox
(Fox fox fox fox fox fox fox)
"THANKS FOR THE SONG!
I'LL SEE YOU AROUND
SO LONG!"

THE BOY WHO CRIED WOLF

To begin with, the boy liked looking after the sheep. He played all day, and no one stopped him and told him to feed the chickens or gather the eggs or chop the wood. He blew on his whistle and danced with the lambs as they frisked and skipped in the long, lush grass. He scratched his dog's head and threw sticks for her to chase. In the evenings he and the dog drove the flock across the hill to meet up with the other shepherds, and they lay down together beside a roaring fire to sleep.

After a while, however, the boy grew bored.

"It's no FUN up here on my own," he grumbled. "There's no one to talk to. No one takes any notice of me. All the sheep do is chew, chew, chew . . ." He blew a sad little tune on his pipe. "Even the lambs are too big to dance any more. And there's no sign of a fox or a wolf or a big brown bear . . ."

The boy stopped. He looked at the sheep grazing quietly among the summer flowers. He looked at his dog dozing in the sunshine. He looked away to where the other shepherds were sitting peacefully with their flocks. He looked down at the little village in the hollow of the hill beneath him. Men and women and children were moving calmly and slowly about their work.

"It's all so DULL," said the boy. "So DULL!" And he jumped to his feet.

The sheep raised their heads. The dog opened her eyes.

"WOOOOOOOOOOOOOOOOOOOOOOOOLF!" yelled the boy at the top of his voice.

"WOOOOOOOOOOOOOOOOOOOOOOOOOLF! HELP! HELP!" And he ran round and round and in and out of the sheep until they were all scurrying this way and that in fright.

"BAAAAAAAAAAAAH!" they bleated. "BAAAAAAAAAAAAH!"

16

The dog barked loudly, and the nearby shepherds snatched at their sticks and came hurrying to help him. Down in the village everybody dropped what they were doing and came streaming up the hill.

"Where is it?" they asked. "Where's the wolf? Is it big? Is it fierce? Has it taken any sheep?"

The boy leaned on his stick. "I drove it away!" he said. "It was huge and grey and hungry, but I drove it away!"

Everybody cheered. The boy was hugged and fussed and patted and petted, and the next day his older brother stayed with him. But after that the brother went back to the village, and the boy was left alone again. He sighed as he saw his brother vanish away down the hill.

"That was fun," he said.

The boy looked after his sheep for another week. He whistled his tunes, and he threw sticks for his dog, but he did not feel like playing and dancing.

"It's so DULL," he said, and he rubbed his nose and thought. "H'm," he said, and looked around. There were the shepherds tending their sheep, and the people of the village working below, just as they always were.

"WOOOOOOOOOOOOOOOOOOOOOOOOLF!" shouted the boy, and he clapped his hands so that the startled sheep hustled and bustled against each other.

"WOOOOOOOOOOOOOOOOOOOOOOOLF!"

The sheep bleated loudly. The dog barked. The shepherds came running. The people of the village hurried up the steep path puffing and panting.

"Where is it? Where's the wolf?" they shouted.

The boy shook his head. "It must have slipped away when it heard you," he said.

The people and the shepherds looked at each other, and several shook their heads. The boy was hugged and told he was brave, but no one stayed with him. Quite soon he was alone again on the hill.

"Come on," he said crossly to his dog. "Let's round up the sheep."

The boy looked after his sheep for another three days. He didn't play his whistle, and he hardly spoke to his dog.

"Sheep are dull," he said. "Everything's DULL."

The dog wagged her tail, but the boy took no notice.

"Let's have some FUN," he said, and he jumped to his feet.

"WOOOOOOOOOOOOOOOOOOOOOOOOOOLF!" he shouted,

"WOOOOOOOOOOOOOOOOOOOOOOOOOOLF!"

Even the sheep hardly moved. The dog got slowly to her feet, and a couple of the shepherds came running. A few villagers puffed up the path, but they didn't seem surprised when the boy explained that the HUGE wolf had already vanished. They nodded, and winked at each other before they went back home.

That evening the sky was heavy with dark grey clouds. The boy was thinking it was time to move his sheep across the hill when the dog suddenly began to growl. He looked at her, surprised, and saw that her fur was bristling and her teeth were bared.

"What is it, Dog?" he asked.

The sheep were moving restlessly.

"BAAAAAH!" they bleated anxiously.
"BAAAAAAAAAAAAH!"

And then the boy saw it. A slinking, sliding grey shadow, creeping and crouching as it slipped nearer and and nearer.

"WOOOOOOOOOOOOOOOOOOOOOOLF!" he yelled.

"WOOOOOOOOOOOOOOOOOOOOOOLF!"

No one came. The boy yelled again, and again, and again. The dog growled one last growl, and then whimpered and scampered away, her tail between her legs.

"WOOOOOOOOOOOOOOOOOOOOOOLF!" the boy screamed and screeched, but still no one answered. With a loud wail he ran for the nearest tree and heaved himself up.

The wolf sprang.

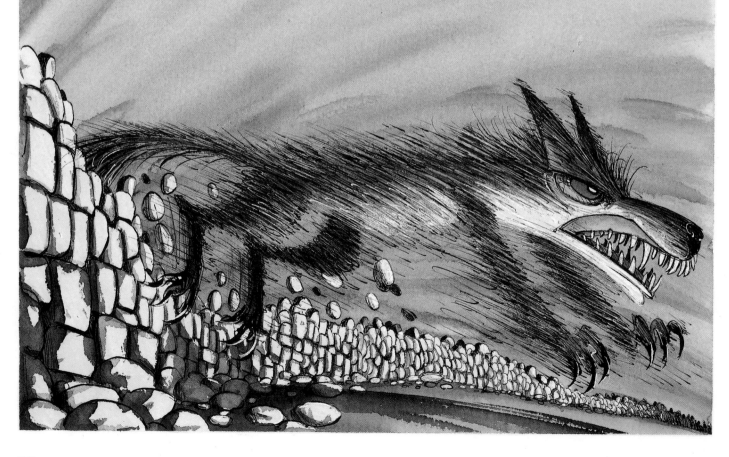

By morning there were no sheep left. Only the boy, sitting in his tree. When the shepherds came to see why he hadn't come to the fire the night before they saw what had happened.

"I'll never cry Wolf again!" the boy sobbed.

"No," said the shepherds, "you won't." And they sent him back down to the village, where he fed the chickens and gathered the eggs and chopped the wood . . . and never had time to play.

THE LION AND THE MOUSE

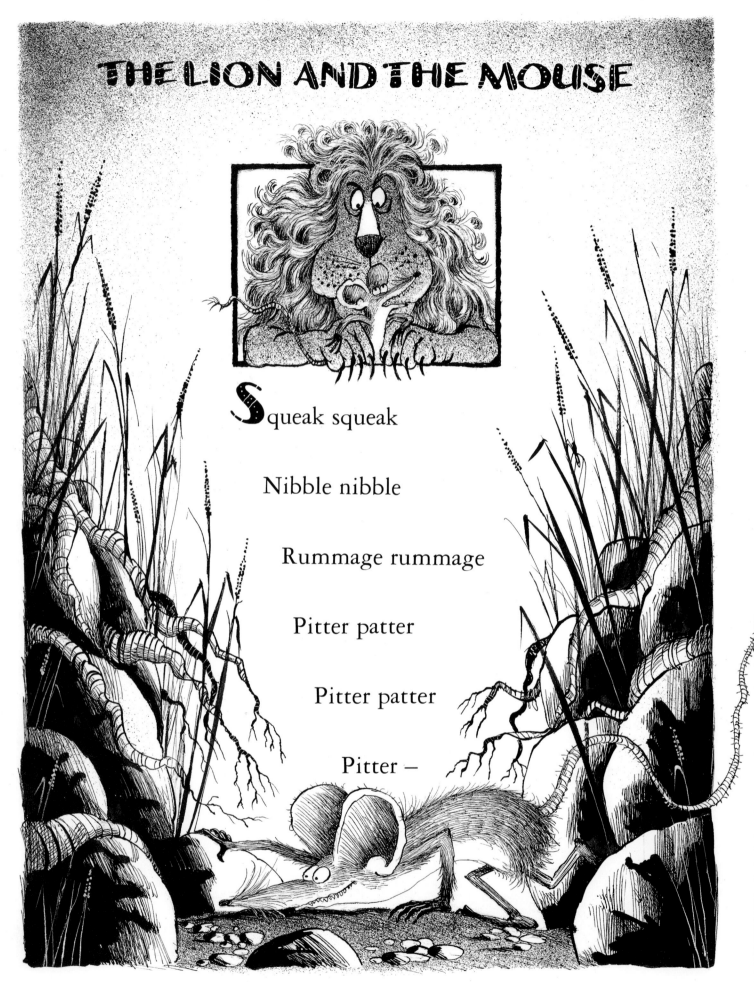

Squeak squeak

Nibble nibble

Rummage rummage

Pitter patter

Pitter patter

Pitter —

EEEEEEEEEEEEEEEEEEEEEEEEEEEEEK!

Oh no no no no no no no!

Oh my pitter patter heart oh my whiskers
That are trembling!

Mr Lion

Please don't eat me!

Let me go!

Oh goodness me

Oh Mr Lion
As I hurry as I scurry to my hole, to my house

I'll be squeaking I'll be dancing I'll be prancing,
I'll be singing you

The thanks of a mouse.

Squeak squeak

Nibble nibble

Rummage rummage

Pitter patter

Pitter patter

Pitter –

EEEEEEEEEEEEEEEEEEEEEEEEEEEK!

Mr Lion!

Are you caught?
Is the net wound around you are you tricked
Are you trapped?

Is the rope long and strong does it hold you
To the ground?

Oh, Mr Lion

Your paws are raw with tearing and your voice
Is hoarse from roaring

There are tears in your eyes.

Do not weep.

No, do not weep.

I will creep I will nibble I will bite I will chew

And little

By little
By little

I will chew right through

All the ropes

Until you

Are free

Like me.

There you go, Mr Lion!

No need for thanks.

Squeak Squeak

Nibble nibble

Rummage rummage

Pitter patter

Pitter patter

Pitter pat.

THE FOX AND THE STORK

Fox was making soup – a mouth-watering, nose-twitching, stomach-filling soup.

"H'm! A pinch of salt," he said to himself, "just one more pinch of salt and it'll be done. OH! How I shall ENJOY my soup! How I shall SLURP my soup! How I shall SMACK my lips and RUB my stomach!"

Fox stopped stirring. "What a shame there is no one to admire my magnificent cooking! Maybe I should invite someone to share my soup and dine with me."

Fox sat down to think. "I won't ask Lion," he decided, "because Lion would gobble all the soup at a gulp, and there would be none left for me. And I won't invite Dog or Cat because they would eat at least half. And I won't invite Bluebottle because of her buzz. Besides, she would put her feet in the food."

Fox went on thinking. "H'm. H'm. H'm. I know!" He leaped up.

"I'll invite my dear friend Stork! Stork is a bird of fine feathers and feelings – Stork will be the ideal guest!" And Fox went hurrying out to invite his friend.

Stork was pleased to come. She bowed in the doorway, and thanked Fox for his kindness.

"What a DELICIOUS smell! Mr Fox, what a wonderful cook you must be. I am most honoured to be asked to share your soup!"

Fox bowed back, and he grinned a foxy grin. As he bowed he was thinking snidy slidy foxy thoughts . . .

"Aha!" he said to himself. "Mrs Stork loves the SMELL of my soup! But if she loves the TASTE she might eat too long and too well! Let me see . . . Let me see . . . AHA!"

Fox hurried to set the table. He set a wide flat dish for himself, and a wide flat dish for Mrs Stork. Mrs Stork watched him, and her shiny little black eyes winked and blinked as she saw what Fox was doing.

"Do be seated, dear friend," Fox said, and he began to ladle the soup on to the plates. "Such hot soup! But you will find it cools quickly. See! I can eat mine now!" And Fox lapped up his soup with a flourish. "Aaaaaah! SO delicious!"

Mrs Stork could eat nothing. Her long bill clicked and clacked against the dish, but not a drop of soup could she drink.

"DEAR Mrs Stork!" Fox said. "Aren't you hungry? Dear me, dear me. Allow me to finish your soup for you . . . waste not, want not, after all!"

Fox drank up Mrs Stork's soup with a loud slurp. Then he licked out the pan and polished the plates with his long red tongue.

"THERE!" said Fox. He sat back, his stomach bulging, and smacked his lips.

"Dear Mrs Stork," he said, "there is nothing as fine as sharing a meal with a friend." And he smiled his foxy smile.

Mrs Stork nodded. "You are quite right, Mr Fox," she said. "Indeed, you are right . . . so I hope you will join me for a meal tonight. It would give me such pleasure to return your kindness!"

Fox shuffled a little and pulled at his whiskers. His slippery thoughts slid round in his head. Was Mrs Stork staring a little coldly with her bright shining eyes? But a free meal was a free meal . . . and there was no soup left. Not a drip or a drop.

"I shall be delighted," Fox said.

Mrs Stork bowed once more in the doorway.

"Until tonight," she said. "And the pleasure will be all mine."

By the evening Fox was hungry again. He leaped out of his house and trotted through the deep dark woods to Mrs Stork's house. A wonderful smell was wafting out through the open window.

Fox sniffed happily, and rubbed his stomach. "TWO fine dinners in a day!" he said, and knocked at the door.

Mrs Stork smiled as she let Fox in.

"DO sit down, dear friend," she said.

Fox hurried to the table. He stopped, and stared.

The table was heaped high with mouth-watering, nose-twitching, stomach-filling food . . . but every dish was tall and narrow.

"Just help yourself, dear friend!" said Mrs Stork. "Feel free to eat whatever you wish!" and she plunged her long thin beak into the tallest bowl.

Fox said nothing. His stomach was howling and growling with hunger, but Fox said nothing at all.

"DEAR Mr Fox!" said Mrs Stork. "Aren't you hungry? What a shame. What a shame. Allow me to finish the meal for you."

And she did.

THE HARE AND THE TORTOISE

Oh me
(Plod plod)
Oh my
(Plod plod)
Could it be
That I spy
Hare over there?

Tortoise!

Tortoise!

Hi! Hi! Hi! Hi! Hi!

(Dash rush bounce rush dash)

Hi! Hi! Hi! Hi! Hi!

Are you crawling are you creeping

Could it be that you are sleeping?

I can hop and skip and bound

While you plod along the ground

See me here!

See me there!

I am spinning everywhere!

Well well

(Trudge trudge)

Now now

(Trudge trudge)

That may be so.

But let me tell you, Hare

I may be slow

(Trudge trudge)

But I am steady.

Steady.

Steady.

Tortoise!
See me dance!
See me spin!
Any race
I can win!
I am faster than the birds
Than the breeze
Than the wind
I can leave them all behind!

Aha.
(Stump stump)
Oho.
(Stump stump)
We'll see.
Yes.
We'll see.
Hare!
I challenge you!
Hare!
Race me!

What what what?
(Gasp gasp)
RACE YOU?
RACE A TORTOISE?

That's right, Hare.
(Sniff)
Race me!

Goodness me.
We can race we can run
But it won't be any fun
I can leap and run so fast
That I know you will be last
One two three are you ready?
One two three are you steady?
One two three here we go!
(Dash rush bounce rush dash)

Plod plod
Trudge trudge
Stump stump.

Here I go here I go here I go!
When I leap I almost fly
Like an arrow through the sky
When I hop and skip and bound
My feet barely touch the ground . . .

Plod plod
Trudge trudge
Stump stump.
Here I go here I go . . .

The winning post's in sight
(Yawn)
I really think I might . . .
(Yawn yawn)
Have a snooze . . .

Plod plod
Trudge trudge
Stump stump.

Sssssssssssnore . . . .
Sssssssssssnore . . . .
Sssssssssssnore . . . .

Oh me

(Plod plod)

Oh my

(Plod plod)

Could it be

That I spy Hare

Over there?

(Trudge trudge)

Could it be that I am creeping

Right past Hare as he is sleeping?

Tee hee!

(Trudge trudge)

Tee hee!

I may be slow

(Stump stump)

But I am steady.

Steady.

Steady.

The winning post's in sight
I really think I might
(Stump stump)
Win!!!!!!!!

What what what . . .
(Yawn stretch)
WHAT WHAT WHAT??????

While Hare slept in the sun
Guess what?
Tortoise won!

THE JACKDAW AND THE PIGEONS

"Coo, coo, coo!" sang the pigeons in the yard.
"Coo, coo, coo! We are fat, we are fed, we are full, we
are happy! Oh, how happy we are!"

Jackdaw was sitting on the fence and watching.
He saw the pearl-grey pigeons flutter and fluff and
preen as they waddled and paddled to and fro. He saw
their dish of water sparkling in the sunshine. He saw
the farmer's wife come out and toss handfuls of
gleaming yellow corn on to the ground.

"Caw," said Jackdaw to himself. "Fancy that! What a life! Why, they don't even hurry to peck up their corn! Caw! CAW!" And he hopped down to share the pigeons' breakfast.

FLAP and FLUTTER! SQUAWK and SCREECH! The pigeons fell over each other in their hurry to scuttle and scurry away. The farmer's wife came out of the kitchen door waving a wooden spoon and shouting "Shoo! Shoo! Get away! Horrid bird! Get away!"

Jackdaw went back to his fence to think. Such an easy life being a pigeon! Such a cold, hard life being a jackdaw. Pigeons were such foolish, fluttery, waddling birds. Jackdaw was sharp and bright and clever . . .

Jackdaw winked his shiny black eye. Jackdaw lifted his wings and flew. Jackdaw flew with long strong beats of his shimmering black feathers all the way to the clay pit. He rolled and he ducked and he dived in the soft clay, and when he came out he was as pearly grey as any pigeon.

"CAW!" said Jackdaw. "Caw! How clever I am! And now for breakfast and dinner and tea!"

The farmer's wife never noticed the extra bird fluttering and preening among the pigeons in the yard. The pigeons cooed and waddled and paddled to and fro, Jackdaw among them.

"Here you are, my pretties!" called the farmer's wife as the sun began to sink. "Here you are, my loves, my doves, my pretty ones!" And she tossed handfuls of corn from the kitchen door.

"Coo! Coo! Coo!" sang the pigeons.

"CAW! CAW! CAW!" squawked Jackdaw.

"AAAAAAAAGH!" screeched the farmer's wife. She rushed out, waving her wooden spoon. "SHOO! SHOO! SHOO!"

There was nothing Jackdaw could do except flap and stagger away, his wings clogged with clay. He half flew, half scrambled over the fence, and dragged

himself along until he found a flock of jackdaws
scratching among the grit and gravel at the side of
the path.

"CAW!" said Jackdaw. "What SILLY birds
pigeons are!"

The jackdaws turned on him.

"And WHAT are you?" asked the oldest jackdaw.
"You're not one of us! Shoo! Shoo!" And all the other
jackdaws joined in.

"Nasty dirty grey bird! Shoo! Shoo! Get away!
Get away!"

Jackdaw waddled slowly away to have a bath . . .

THE DOG AND THE BONE

Once
There
Was
A
Dog
Who
Was greedy graspy always wanting everything himself.
And
He
Found
A
Bone
That

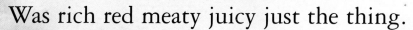

Was rich red meaty juicy just the thing.
"MINE!" said the dog.
"ALL MINE!"
And he picked up the bone in his snappy snarly teeth
      and ran.

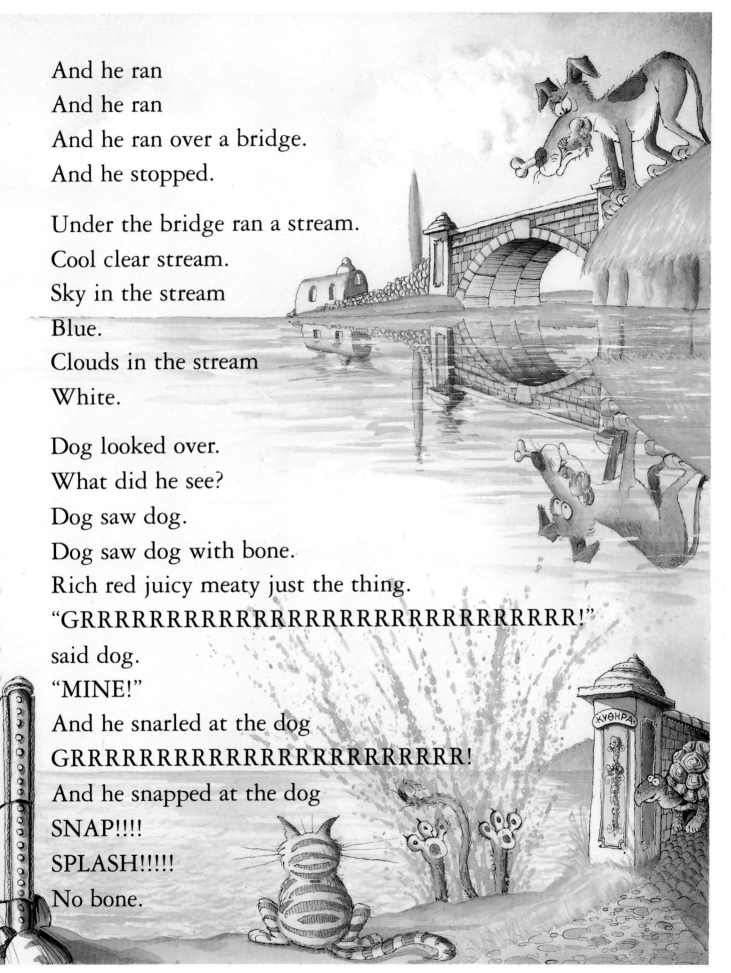

And he ran
And he ran
And he ran over a bridge.
And he stopped.

Under the bridge ran a stream.
Cool clear stream.
Sky in the stream
Blue.
Clouds in the stream
White.

Dog looked over.
What did he see?
Dog saw dog.
Dog saw dog with bone.
Rich red juicy meaty just the thing.
"GRRRRRRRRRRRRRRRRRRRRRRRRRRRRR!"
said dog.
"MINE!"
And he snarled at the dog
GRRRRRRRRRRRRRRRRRRRRRR!
And he snapped at the dog
SNAP!!!!
SPLASH!!!!!
No bone.

THE BAT, THE BRAMBLE AND THE CORMORANT

There were once three friends, and very good friends they were. They met every day and Cormorant would tell his friends stories, wonderful stories about the sea and the winds and the rolling waves, and Bat and Bramble held their breath and asked for more and more.

It was after one of Cormorant's stories that Bat had his idea.

"Why," he squeaked, "you know all there is to know about the sea. We could make our fortunes! We could choose a ship, and send goods away to be bought and sold in foreign parts . . . and then we could live like kings and queens with the gold that our trading brings us!"

Cormorant stood up and bowed. Bramble curtsied.

"My dear friend," said Cormorant, "what a wonder you are!"

"How true, how true!" said Bramble. "But couldn't we all go too? I have always had a longing to travel."

Bat flapped his wings in delight. "Oh YES!" he squeaked. "What fun, what fun!"

The three friends began to get ready for their great adventure. Bat went into the towns and cities and borrowed gold and silver. "I shall take my money with me and buy fine silks and satins in far distant lands," he squeaked. "Then I shall bring them home, and sell them here for so much gold that I will never need to work again."

Bramble nodded. "You may be right, dear Bat. I have decided to buy good woollen cloth to take away; there is nothing like good woollen cloth. I am sure that I will do excellently well from selling my cloth."

Cormorant stood on one leg. "Well," he said, "I have bought boxes of brass pots and pans. Everyone likes to buy pots and pans. It seems to me that I will be the richest of all of us."

Bat and Bramble looked at him, and then at each other.

"We shall see," squeaked Bat.

"Indeed we will," said Bramble.

At last a ship was found: a strong and sturdy ship that flew a brightly coloured flag at her mast.

"She will slither and slide over the roughest of waves," said Cormorant.

"She will carry us to our fortunes!" squeaked Bat.

Bramble said nothing. She knew nothing about ships.

The three adventurers went on board. Bat was carrying his bags of gold and silver. Bramble had already ordered the sailors to carry her good woollen cloth on to the deck. Cormorant's boxes of brass pots and pans were safe in the ship's hold.

The sailors hauled up the anchor, the ship's sails bellied out and filled with wind, and she flew over the seas.

Cormorant strode around the deck. "A good breeze!" he said. "We will soon reach land again!"

But as the day went on the breeze became a gust, and the gust became a gale. The sailors hurried to reef in the sails, but the ship was blown wildly off course.

CRASH!

The ship struck a rock. She staggered, and cracked in two. Cormorant and Bat were just in time to fly up into the hissing sheets of wind and hail as the ship reeled and sank beneath the foaming waves. Bramble floated up and over the pounding waves until she found herself washed up on the shore.

"Oh, my fortune! My fortune!" she wailed. "Oh, my good woollen cloth! My woollen cloth!"

Cormorant and Bat, wind-beaten and bedraggled, flapped and flopped down beside her.

"All is lost!" sighed Cormorant. "All is lost!"

"I'll never go to sea again! Never!" Bat squeaked miserably.

By the following morning the storm had died down, and the sea was calm again. The three travellers found that they were not too far from home, but not one of them wished to go back.

"Maybe," said Cormorant, "maybe my brass pots and pans will wash up on the shore. I will watch, and search, and peek under stones and rocks." And he stalked up and down the sea's edge, day after day after day . . . and so did all cormorants after him.

Bramble settled herself by the edge of the shore. As men and women and children walked and skipped and hopped past her to the beach she pulled and tugged with her thorny fingers at their clothes . . . day after day after day.

"You see," she said to Cormorant, "it could be my good woollen cloth they are wearing. It could, indeed."

"Perhaps so," said Cormorant . . . and he saw that all brambles grew long thorny fingers and clutched and tugged just like his dear friend.

Bat was not seen by day. He was afraid that the rich city and town dwellers who had lent him their silver and gold would come hunting for him, so he began to fly only at night.

"Eeek!" he squeaked sadly, as he flew in circles night after night after night. "Eeek!"

"Eeek!" called all the other bats. "Eeek!" And they too flew round and round and round and round . . . night after night after night.

THE WOLF AND THE CRANE

Gobble gobble gobble gobble gobble gobble crunch!

Wolf was eating
Wolf was munching
Wolf was tearing
Wolf was crunching
When . . .

      "OW!"

"Ow ow ow!" said Wolf
"I've swallowed a bone."
Wolf shook his head
And he opened his jaws wide
And he shook his head
And he ran to the stream to drink
And he shook his head . . .
And he shook his head . . .
And he shook his head . . .

BUT . . .
"OW! OW! OW!" howled Wolf
"There's a bone in my throat and I can't get it out and
it HURTS!"

Flap! Flap! Flap!
A flight of cranes flew by.
Flap! Flap! Flap!
And Wolf looked up.

Wolf sat down and thought.
"Mr Crane," Wolf thought. "Oh ho!"
"Oh ho!" Wolf thought. "Of course!
His beak
Is long
His beak
Is narrow
His beak
Can tweak
And pick
And PULL that bone
Right out of my throat!"

Wolf went hurrying through the woods.
Pant pant hurry scurry hurry scurry.
"Mr Crane!
Mr Crane!
With your beak
Will you tweak this bone from my throat?"

Mr Crane shook his head.
"Oh no.
Not me.
Your teeth are far too sharp
Your teeth are far too strong
Your teeth are gleaming white and much too long
Oh no.
Not me."

Wolf sighed. Wolf scratched. Wolf thought.
Wolf rolled on his back.
"Dear Mr Crane
Kind Mr Crane
I'll give you silver and I'll give you gold
And a wife to care for you when you're old
Dear Mr C.
Kind Mr C.
Just do this one little thing for me!"

"H'm," said Mr Crane and his eyes shone.

"H'm," said Mr Crane and he hopped forward.

"H'm," said Mr Crane

"H'm . . .

Do you promise?"

"I promise," said Wolf. "Oh, I do I do I do!

By the sun and the moon and the stars in the sky

Cross my heart and hope to die!"

"Very well," said Crane
And he picked and he pulled
With his long narrow beak
And he gave a tweak
And the bone was out.

All gone.

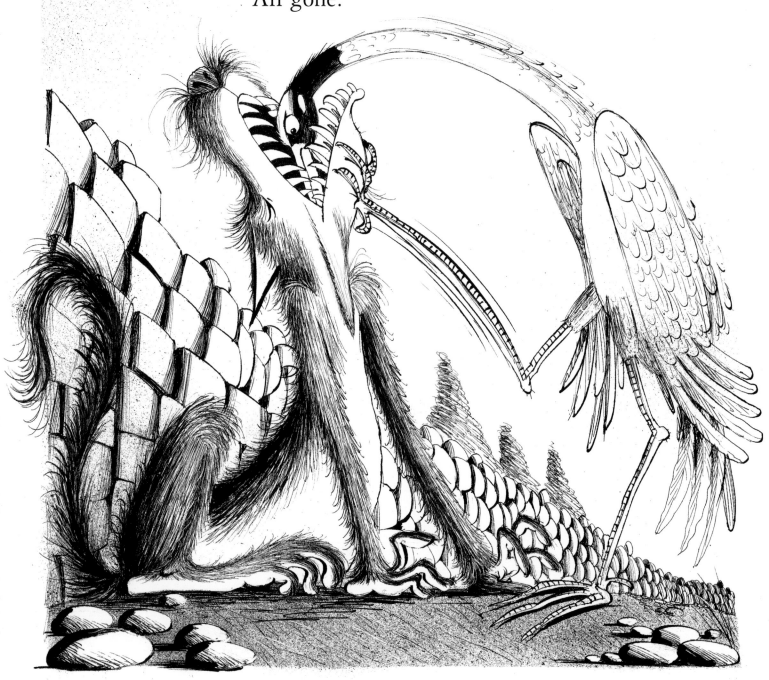

"There! Mr Wolf," said Crane
"Now where's my silver? Where's my gold?
My wife to care for me when I'm old?"

Wolf growled.
Wolf snarled.
Wolf flashed his teeth.
"Flip flap away, Mr Crane!
You put your head in the jaws of a wolf
And you'll never do that again
Flip! Flap! Fly away! Or the bones in my throat
Will all be the bones of a crane!"

THE TRAVELLER AND THE BEAR

"Twinkle twinkle, little stars!"
Sang the man as he walked with the bear.
"Twinkle twinkle, little stars!
Can you see the stars in the velvet sky?
See them watching us, you and I!"

The bear said nothing.
The bear padded on, watching the rough and stony
   ground beneath his feet.
The trees whispered and murmured in the night
And dark shadows lay across the way.
The bear padded on, and on, and on.

"Hey there, bear! Look up and see
See how the stars wink down at me!
Why do you stare at the dank dark ground?
The heavens are glittering all around . . ."

And still the bear looked down . . .
And still the bear padded on, and on, and on . . .

75

"Look up! Look up to the sparkling sky
Or the stars will laugh as you pass them by –"

CRASH!!!!!!!!!!!!!!

SPLASH!!!!!!!!!!!!!

Roly poly roly poly roly poly into the ditch.

The bear looked up and he shook his head.
"There's a time", he said, "for looking at stars
And a time to look at the road ahead."

The man muttered
And sputtered his way out of the ditch.
"If ever the stars were laughing
They're laughing now," he said.